I'm Going To READ!™

These levels are meant only
you and your child can best choose

Level 1: Kindergarten–Grade 1 . . . Ages 4–6
- word bank to highlight new words
- consistent placement of text to promote readability
- easy words and phrases
- simple sentences build to make simple stories
- art and design help new readers decode text

Level 2: Grade 1 . . . Ages 6–7
- word bank to highlight new words
- rhyming texts introduced
- more difficult words, but vocabulary is still limited
- longer sentences and longer stories
- designed for easy readability

Level 3: Grade 2 . . . Ages 7–8
- richer vocabulary of up to 200 different words
- varied sentence structure
- high-interest stories with longer plots
- designed to promote independent reading

Level 4: Grades 3 and up . . . Ages 8 and up
- richer vocabulary of more than 300 different words
- short chapters, multiple stories, or poems
- more complex plots for the newly independent reader
- emphasis on reading for meaning

LEVEL 2

Library of Congress Cataloging-in-Publication Data Available

10   9

Published by Sterling Publishing Co., Inc.
387 Park Avenue South, New York, NY 10016
Text copyright © 2005 by Harriet Ziefert Inc.
Illustrations copyright © 2005 by Rich Rossi
Distributed in Canada by Sterling Publishing
c/o Canadian Manda Group, 165 Dufferin Street,
Toronto, Ontario, Canada M6K 3H6
Distributed in the United Kingdom by GMC Distribution Services,
Castle Place, 166 High Street, Lewes, East Sussex, England BN7 1XU
Distributed in Australia by Capricorn Link (Australia) Pty. Ltd.
P.O. Box 704, Windsor, NSW 2756, Australia

Printed in China

Sterling ISBN-13: 978-1-4027-2719-1

For information about custom editions, special sales, premium and
corporate purchases, please contact Sterling Special Sales
Department at 800-805-5489 or specialsales@sterlingpub.com.

Pillow Fight

Pictures by Richard Rossi

STERLING
New York / London
www.sterlingpublishing.com/kids

**Mike and Tony
were buddies.**

They walked to school together.

They ate lunch together.

**Mike picked Tony
for his team.**

And Tony picked Mike.

**After school
they played ball . . .**

and tag . . .

and leapfrog.

Sometimes they rode bikes.

And sometimes they did nothing much at all.

**On Friday nights Mike and
Tony had sleepovers.**

They took turns getting cookies.

They took turns calling their friends.

**One Friday night Mike and Tony
had a pillow fight.**

**It was a small pillow
fight that grew . . .**

and grew . . .

and grew!

**Mike and Tony threw
down their pillows.**

They grabbed each other.
Mike sat on Tony.

And Tony sat on Mike.
Tony yelled, "I win!"

**Mike shouted, "You did not!
You cheated!"**

bag   door   ran

**Mike took his sleeping bag
and ran out the door.**

Tony called his mother.
"Mike ran away!"

"Let's go find him,"
said Tony's mother.

When Tony found Mike,
Mike yelled, "You didn't win!"

"Okay! Okay!" said Tony.
"I didn't win. Nobody did."

**Mike and Tony
were buddies again.**